Witch

Steve Barlow and Steve Skidmore
Illustrated by Judit Tondora

Franklin Watts
First published in Great Britain in 2019 by The Watts Publishing Group

Text © Steve Barlow and Steve Skidmore 2019
Illustrations by Judit Tondora © Franklin Watts 2019
The "2Steves" illustration by Paul Davidson
used by kind permission of Orchard Books

PB ISBN 978 1 4451 6966 8
ebook ISBN 978 1 4451 6967 5
Library ebook ISBN 978 1 4451 6968 2

1 3 5 7 9 10 8 6 4 2

Printed in Great Britain

Franklin Watts
An imprint of
Hachette Children's Group
Part of The Watts Publishing Group
Carmelite House
50 Victoria Embankment
London EC4Y 0DZ

An Hachette UK Company
www.hachette.co.uk

www.franklinwatts.co.uk

How to be a hero

This book is not like others you have read. This is a choose-your-own-destiny book where YOU are the hero of this adventure.

Each section of this book is numbered. At the end of most sections, you will have to make a choice. Each choice will take you to a different section of the book.

If you choose correctly, you will succeed. But be careful. If you make a bad choice, you may have to start the adventure again. If this happens, make sure you learn from your mistake!

Go to the next page to start your adventure. And remember, don't be a zero, be a hero!

You are an apprentice witch at the Academy for Modern Witches.

You have been training for several years and hope to become a fully qualified member of the Circle of Witches. This is a secret society that uses magic for good to help protect the world against the dark forces that are out there.

You spend hours every day learning complicated spells and potions.

Recently you decided to use your magical powers to help an old lady find her lost cat. You know that you shouldn't have done this without permission and now Mistress Weathervane, the Head Teacher of the Academy, has summoned you to her office.

You stand outside her door, feeling very nervous...

Go to 1.

1

The door swings open and a voice rings out.

"Enter!"

You walk in. The door slams shut behind you.

You see Mistress Weathervane floating above her chair.

"Did you use magic to open the door?" you ask.

"Of course not," she replies. "I used electricity. It's an automatic door. This is the 21st century and there's no point using up magic when we can use technology!"

She floats down back into her chair.

"Do you know why I have summoned you here?"

To pretend that you don't, go to 26.
To admit that you do, go to 45.

2

You point your wand at the banshee.
"Destroy!" you order. Nothing happens.

The banshee cackles. "I warned you,
witch. Old magic will not work against me!"

She raises her hand and you are lifted
into the air. "Now, join your sisters in The
Dark Realm forever!"

She sends you hurtling towards the glass.
You only have a split second to act!

Go to 23.

3

"Avoid!" you order. The skateboard banks to
the right at incredible speed.

But the genies also speed up. One moves
to your right and the other to your left.
They are outflanking you. You will have to
use magic!

**To let the wand decide which spell to
cast, go to 28.**

To cast a destruction spell, go to 32.

4

You recall Mistress Weathervane's warning about using magic without permission. "I'm sorry," you say. "I'm already in trouble for helping you..."

"You must listen to me," she replies. "I'm not who you think I am."

Go to 22.

5

You dive behind a table as the door opens.

As you stare at the lift, you feel something grasping at your leg. You look back and see a half-dissolved gingerbread man enveloping your body! Before you can react, a gingery arm grabs your wand, pulling it into its soggy mush!

You are trapped.

Go to 23.

6

You realise that these flowers are hexed to resist magical intruders! If you cast any more spells with the wand you will set off more explosions.

You decide to head to the front entrance.

Go to 20.

7

"What is this task?" you ask.

Mother Oak takes out a crystal ball from her bag.

"Is that a real one?" you say. "I've never seen one before. We just use the Crystal Ball app."

"Hmmm..." Mother Oak shakes her head. "Look into it..."

You do and see your classmates and teachers — they seem to be in a trance-like state behind a dark glass.

"I believe they have been imprisoned in The Dark Realm by Elias Midnight. I think he is a warlock.

The trip to Tempest Towers was a trap. I tried to warn Mistress Weathervane, but she wouldn't listen to an old witch like me. You are the only witch left who can defeat Elias Midnight and rescue your sisters."

"But what about you?" you ask.

"I am too old and frail. It needs a young witch like you. Will you accept this task?"

To accept the task, go to 49.

To ask more questions about your task, go to 42.

8

"Turn!" you cry. The broomstick spins to the left, but the cloud simply mirrors your movement and continues closing in on you.

Again you try to manoeuvre out of the way, but the cloud changes course. You decide to head straight for it!

Go to 47.

"Destroy!" you cry. But your wand just transforms into a bunch of flowers!

"What are you doing?" says Elias Midnight.

Without your wand you are at Elias's mercy! You turn to Miss Devine.

"Help me!"

"I can't," she says.

There's only one way out of this situation!

Go to 23.

10

"It's not fair to punish me when I..."

But before you can finish, Mistress Weathervane flicks her hand and a small rainbow appears in the air. It wraps itself around your mouth, stifling your protests.

"I decide what is fair," she snaps. "Is that understood?"

"Mmm... mmm," you mumble.

"Good." She drops her hand and the rainbow disappears.

Go to 35.

11

You know there is no time to waste so you ignore the table of goodies. As you step past it there is a crash of thunder and a roar of wind. When it subsides, you are amazed to see an army of giant gingerbread people crunching towards you!

Before you can move away, one topples down on you and you crash to the floor, unconscious.

Go to 29.

12

"Invisible," you say. You feel a tingling in your body and look down at your hands — you can't see them!

You step forward past the guards and dogs, but as you do you hear a low growl. You are amazed as the dogs begin to transform into creatures from your worst nightmares!

They have the head of a human, the body of a lion and the tail of a scorpion. You recognise these supernatural beasts. Manticores! They cannot be fooled by invisibility spells. They move, leading the guards towards you.

To run to the entrance, go to 16.

To use magic against the manticores, go to 41.

13

You head to the academy's broom cupboard and choose an old broomstick.

Sitting astride it, you order the broomstick to go to Tempest Towers. You shoot out of the window and zoom across rooftops. As you get nearer to Elias Midnight's headquarters, you see a dark cloud ahead of you. You are amazed — it is speeding straight towards you!

To take evasive action, go to 8.

To carry on, go to 47.

14

"You're going to swap places with my sisters," you say. The phones and wand burst into life and their combined magical forces send the banshee hurtling towards the dark glass.

There is a shattering noise and the room is suddenly full of witches! Then the glass re-forms and behind it you see the banshee mouthing curses at you.

Mistress Weathervane stares at you in astonishment. "What's been going on here?" she asks.

You smile. "It's a long story!"

Go to 50.

"Skywards," you command, and the skateboard obeys, shooting up into the air. In seconds you are zigzagging through skyscrapers at top speed, heading for Elias Midnight's HQ.

Ahead you see a large black cloud. You are surprised to see it moving towards you.

To use your wand to investigate the cloud, go to 40.

To carry on, go to 47.

16

You race towards the entrance, but the manticores are too quick. With a huge leap, one of the supernatural creatures smashes into your back and you crash to the ground.

Your wand spins out of your hand. The other manticores move in, tails raised, ready to strike. You have to act quickly!

Go to 23.

17

The next day, you watch the other witches and teachers heading off to Tempest Towers. With a sigh, you begin to clean the classrooms. You can't even use magic to help you as your phone has been taken away.

The day progresses and as the sun sets, you finish mopping the hall floor. At that moment, the doors fling open with a crash and an old woman dressed in black stands in the doorway. It is the old lady you helped to find her cat.

"I need your magical powers again," she says.

To tell her to go away, go to 4.
To talk to her, go to 22.

18

"Fire flames!" you command.

Flames shoot from the wand and hit a gingerbread person. It sets alight, filling the air with the smell of burning biscuit.

Again you point your wand and a further gingerbread person is cooked to a crisp!

You point your wand at another, but as you do so, a huge gingerbread man crashes down on top of you.

You drop to the floor, unconscious.
Go to 29.

19

You head along the streets, skating through the crowds and the traffic.

But you soon realise that you are taking too long. Speed is essential if you are going to save your sisters.

To order the skateboard to go faster, go to 34.

To go skywards, go to 15.

20

You head to the front door, where you see several security officers with fierce-looking guard dogs patrolling the entrance.

You will have to use magic to get inside the building.

To make yourself invisible, go to 12.
To make the guards unable to move, go to 25.

21

"Yes, I'll help," you say.

"He is in his penthouse. We'll head there now." You follow Miss Devine into the lift and you are soon heading up to meet Elias Midnight.

You hold your wand ready for whatever may come.

Go to 27.

22

"I'm not sure I can help you, but come in," you say. "Who are you?"

The old lady steps forward.

"I am Mother Oak."

You gasp. "Not *the* Mother Oak? The most famous leader of all witches?"

Mother Oak smiles. "I was once, but now I am old and frail. The new witches like Mistress Weathervane don't want me and my old magic — they want new magic — smartphones with apps and SpellBook, and the like."

You are confused.

"But if you have magical powers, why did you want my help to find your cat?"

"It was a test. I wanted to see what sort of witch you are. I have a task for you, if you wish to accept it."

To refuse the task, go to 38.
To find out more, go to 7.

23

You grasp the pentacle and cry, "Old magic, help me!"

There is a roar of air and a burst of light as you pass through time and space.

You find yourself back in the hall. Mother Oak looks stern. "You were unwise in your choice. Begin your task again."

To fly to Tempest Towers on a broomstick, go to 13.

To use your magic skateboard, go to 30.

24

You move through the lobby past a table laden with drinks and plates of biscuits. There are two signs on the table:

It's been some time since you've eaten and you're feeling hungry.

To stop for refreshments, go to 31.
To continue your search for your sisters, go to 11.

25

"Immobilise," you command. The wand's magic works immediately, rendering the guards motionless.

You step off the skateboard and walk towards the doors. However, the spell has only made the guards immobile — they can still speak.

"Intruder!" they cry as one. "Destroy!"

You are amazed as the dogs suddenly begin to transform.

Within seconds several fearsome creatures stand growling before you. They all have human heads, the bodies of lions and the tails of scorpions.

You recognise these nightmarish beasts. Manticores! They start moving towards you.

To run to the entrance, go to 16.

To use magic against the manticores, go to 41.

26

"I have no idea," you say.

Mistress Weathervane looks stern.

"Do not lie to me! You know very well that I can tell if someone is lying!"

"Sorry, Mistress Weathervane," you reply, ashamed.

Go to 45.

27

The lift door opens and you step into a huge office.

"We don't want to be disturbed. Put your phone there," says Miss Devine. She points at a table that is covered in mobile phones. You realise they have been taken from your sisters. You are also amazed to see yours.

"I don't have one with me," you reply truthfully. "Where is Elias Midnight?"

The chair behind a huge desk suddenly spins around to reveal a man dressed in black. "I am here. Who are you?"

To attack Elias with magic, go to 9.
To talk to him, go to 39.

28

"Wand, choose a spell and choose it well," you say.

The skateboard comes to a sudden halt as the genies close in from either side, heading directly for you.

A word begins to form in your mind. You wonder what will happen, but shout it nevertheless. "Combine!"

Just as the genies are about to slam into you, the skateboard suddenly shoots forward. The genies cannot stop and hit each other with such incredible force, their bodies join together.

They struggle to break free but the spell is too strong! You speed off laughing.

To head for the front entrance of Tempest Towers, go to 20.

To try to find another way in, go to 44.

29

You wake up to find yourself in the clutch of a gingerbread man. Its mouth is wide open and you're heading towards it! You're about to be eaten by a biscuit!

Go to 23.

30

You decide that using a broomstick is a little old-fashioned, so you head to your locker and take out your magic skateboard.

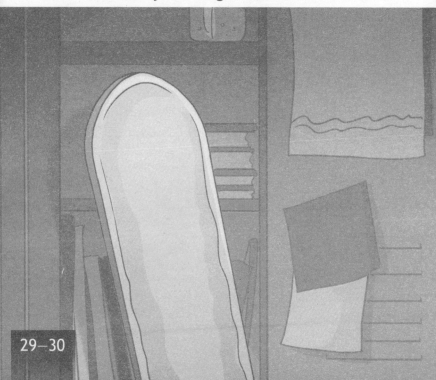

It's lucky Mistress Weathervane didn't know about this, you think as you stand on the board.

"Go!" you order and the skateboard obeys, shooting along the corridors and out of the front gates.

To head to Tempest Towers at street level, go to 19.

To order the skateboard to fly above the city buildings, go to 15.

31

You pick up a biscuit and go to put it in your mouth.

"DON'T YOU DARE!" the biscuit screams, and you drop it. There is a crack of thunder and the biscuits begin to grow! Seconds later there is an army of giant gingerbread people crunching towards you.

You need a spell to deal with these not-so-sweet beings!

To cast a spell of water, go to 48.

To cast a spell of fire, go to 18.

32

You take out your wand but before you can use it, one of the genies unleashes a lightning bolt at you.

It strikes your hand causing the wand to spin from your grasp. The other genie takes hold of your leg. There's only one way out of this dire situation!

Go to 23.

You point at your phone lying on the table. "That is mine. Mistress Weathervane was the last person to have it. She must have brought it here. And the others belong to my sisters. And you're telling me you don't know how they got here?"

Elias shakes his head. "I do not."

You go to pick up your phone.

"DON'T TOUCH IT!" screams Miss Devine. "Or it will go badly for you, witch!"

Miss Devine begins to transform before your eyes into a hideous hag.

"Miss Devine, you're not Miss Devine!" stammers Elias.

"No, you miserable fool, I'm a banshee," screeches the creature. "A sworn enemy of all witches! I've been using you and your company to snare witches and send them to The Dark Realm."

She pulls back a curtain hanging on the wall to reveal a dark piece of glass. You see your sisters trapped behind it, writhing in agony.

You point your wand at the banshee. "Release them or else," you threaten.

She laughs. "Old magic will not work against me!"

If you believe her, go to 43.
If you don't, go to 2.

"Faster," you command.

The skateboard hurtles along the street, barely missing the pedestrians.

Suddenly a huge truck pulls out in front of you.

"Stop!" you cry, but it is too late. You slam into the vehicle. Your wand goes flying and the skateboard is smashed into pieces. You lie on the road, battered and bruised.

You only have one option!

Go to 23.

"Sorry," you say. "I thought I was doing a good deed. What is my punishment?"

"You will not be allowed to go on tomorrow's visit to the Witches Convention at Tempest Towers."

Tempest Towers is the headquarters of Elias Midnight, the founder of Enchantments Incorporated. Each year, witches from around the world visit to see the latest magical fashions, artefacts and potions.

Mistress Weathervane continues, "Instead, you will stay here and clean up the classrooms. I am also confiscating your smartphone with its magical apps until after the convention."

This is another blow. Instead of wands, modern witches have access to magical apps on their phones and without it you cannot perform any spells.

"Now, off you go."

You head out of the office and the door slams shut behind you.

Go to 17.

36

A young woman steps out of the lift.

"Who are you?" she asks.

"Er, I was late for the academy visit," you quickly reply. "I've only just arrived."

"Thank goodness you're here, I need help!" she says. "I'm Miss Devine, Elias Midnight's personal assistant." She gives a sob. "He has been taken over by forces from The Dark Realm. He has done something terrible to your sisters. I tried to stop him, but he is too powerful. I can take you to them, if you promise to help me stop whatever he is planning."

To help Miss Devine, go to 21.
To use magic to test her story, go to 46.

37

"Disappear!" you cry. But more flowers explode. The clouds of pollen grow thicker.

You collapse to the floor. The flowers are hexed to resist intruders! If you cast any more spells, you'll set off more explosions.

Go to 23.

38

"I don't think I should be getting myself into any more trouble..."

Mother Oak's eyes narrow. "If you don't, there will be more trouble in this world than you could ever imagine."

You realise that you need to hear more.

Go to 7.

39

"What have you done with my sisters?" you ask.

Elias Midnight looks puzzled. "I have no idea what you are talking about," he replies. He turns to Miss Devine. "Do you?" he asks.

Miss Devine shakes her head.

"What are those phones doing on the table, then?"

"I have no idea," answers Elias.

To attack Elias with magic, go to 9.
To question him further, go to 33.

40

You bring the skateboard to a halt, point your wand and order, "Reveal!"

Immediately the cloud begins to disintegrate and reveal its true nature. Two genies float in the sky before you! With a roar they head towards you.

To try and outfly the genies, go to 3.
To use your wand, go to 32.

41

Crying, "Transform!" you point your wand at the manticores. A maelstrom of stars spins around the creatures. When it disappears there are three furry kittens in place of the manticores!

The guards look on in disbelief as you hurry towards the entrance. The door slides open and you enter, wave your wand and order, "Barricade!" The doors slam shut. You are in the building.

Go to 24.

"What do I need to do?" you ask.

"You must make your way into Tempest Towers, defeat Elias and rescue your sisters," Mother Oak replies. "This will help you." She hands you a wand. "I know it isn't a modern magic app, but trust in it and the correct magical command will come to you."

She gives you a round, glass pentacle. "This is my magical pentacle. If you are ever in trouble, hold it, call upon the powers of the old magic and it will return you to this time and place, where you can begin your task again."

You take the wand and the pentacle.

"I cannot use magic to teleport you into the building," says Mother Oak. "There is a hex on it. You will have to make your own way there and find a way in."

To fly to Tempest Towers on a broomstick, go to 13.

To use your magic skateboard, go to 30.

"Perhaps not, but maybe this will," you say.

You point your wand at the mobile phones. "Old and new work as one!"

The phones spin into the air and circle the banshee. Magic crackles, spells combine and, as one, blast straight at the hideous creature. The banshee tries to fight back, but is powerless against the force of old and new magic together.

Soon she falls to her knees, exhausted before you. "Enough, witch, you have won."

You call a halt to the magic.

The banshee scowls. "What will you do to me?"

To use your wand to destroy the banshee, go to 2.

To send the banshee into The Dark Realm, go to 14.

44

You reach Tempest Towers and land next to a huge flower bed full of exotic plants and colourful flowers.

You hold out your wand. "Locate a doorway!" you order. But as it does so, the flowers begin to explode, sending thick clouds of pollen into the air.

"Disperse!" you order, but again more flowers explode. The sticky pollen cloud covers you and you begin to choke.

To cast another spell, go to 37.

To get away from the flowers, go to 6.

45

"It's about the lost cat, isn't it?" you say.

"It most certainly is," replies Mistress Weathervane. "You found it using magic without permission."

"But the old lady was so upset," you say. "I had to help."

Mistress Weathervane scowls. "The first rule of this academy is that no trainee witch should use magic in the outside world without permission. Secrecy is everything! I have no choice but to punish you!"

To accept the punishment, go to 35.
To argue against the punishment, go to 10.

46

You point your wand at Miss Devine. But before you can cast the spell, there is a rush of air. You are snatched up in a vortex of wind that spins you around and around.

"No!" screams Miss Devine. "Elias must know you are here! We're doomed!"

Go to 23.

47

You speed towards the cloud and are almost upon it, when it suddenly splits into two. You see it for what it really is — two huge genies!

"Avoid!" you cry. You spin around so quickly that you are almost thrown off your board. You regain balance and zoom away, but the supernatural creatures are fast and they close in on you.

To use your wand, go to 32.
To use your pentacle, go to 23.

48

"Water!" you cry.

A stream of water pours from the wand and hits a gingerbread person. It begins to turn to mush.

Again you point the wand and another blast of water turns a second gingerbread person into a gooey mess. Soon, all of the gingerbread people are victims of your watery wand.

That's a lot of soggy bottoms, you think.

At that moment a lobby lift pings and its doors begin to open.

To hide, go to 5.

To wait and see who or what appears, go to 36.

49

"I'll head to Tempest Towers straight away and rescue my sisters!" you cry.

"Your enthusiasm is to be applauded, but you need to know more," says Mother Oak.

You realise she is right.

Go to 42.

50

You are back in Mistress Weathervane's office. Mother Oak is also present.

"Well, what a story!" exclaims the headmistress. "It seems that there is a place for both old and new magic. Mother Oak was right after all, and so she will be joining our staff next year!"

"What about Elias Midnight?" you ask.

"He knew nothing about the banshee's plans," says Mother Oak. "Under our watchful eye, he'll continue to produce enchantments and potions."

"You saved us all," says Mistress Weathervane. "I'm making you a member of the Circle of Witches! You are a real hero!"

I HERO Quiz

Test yourself with this special quiz. It has been designed to see how much you remember about the book you've just read. Can you get all five answers right?

Question 1

What is the real identity of the old lady you helped?

A   Mistress Weathervane

B   Elias Midnight

C   Miss Devine

D   Mother Oak

Question 2

Where do you find Elias Midnight?

A   Tempest Towers

B   The Academy for Modern Witches

C   The Dark Realm

D   The Circle of Witches

Question 3

What type of magical creature is Miss Devine?

A   a witch

B   a warlock

C   a banshee

D   a genie

Question 4

What is your mission?

A   capture Elias Midnight

B   kill Elias Midnight

C   destroy Tempest Towers

D   rescue your sister witches

Question 5

What do you become a member of?

A   Witches and Wizards Incorporated

B   Witchcraft and Wicca

C   The Temple of Witchcraft

D   The Circle of Witches

About the 2Steves

"The 2Steves" are
one of Britain's
most popular writing
double acts for young
people, specialising
in comedy and
adventure. They
perform regularly in schools and libraries,
and at festivals, taking the power of words
and story to audiences of all ages.

Together they have written many books,
including the *Monster Hunter* series.
Find out what they've been up to at:
www.the2steves.net

About the illustrator: Judit Tondora

Judit Tondora was born in Miskolc, Hungary
and now works from her countryside studio.
Judit's artwork has appeared in books, comics,
posters and on commercial design projects.

To find out more about her work, visit:
**www.astound.us/publishing/artists/
judit-tondora**

Have you completed these I HERO adventures?

Battle with monsters in Monster Hunter:

978 1 4451 5878 5 pb
978 1 4451 5876 1 ebook

978 1 4451 5935 5 pb
978 1 4451 5933 1 ebook

978 1 4451 5936 2 pb
978 1 4451 5937 9 ebook

978 1 4451 5939 3 pb
978 1 4451 5940 9 ebook

978 1 4451 5942 3 pb
978 1 4451 5943 0 ebook

978 1 4451 5945 4 pb
978 1 4451 5946 1 ebook

Defeat all the baddies in Toons:

978 1 4451 5930 0 pb
978 1 4451 5931 7 ebook

978 1 4451 5921 8 pb
978 1 4451 5922 5 ebook

978 1 4451 5924 9 pb
978 1 4451 5925 6 ebook

978 1 4451 5918 8 pb
978 1 4451 5919 5 ebook

Also by the 2Steves...

978 1 4451 5985 0

GALAXY FOOTBALL CUP

STEVE BARLOW ⇒ STEVE SKIDMORE
SANTY GUTIÉRREZ

Tip can't believe his luck when he mysteriously wins tickets to see his favourite team in the cup final. But there's a surprise in store ...

978 1 4451 5892 1

SPACE CHASE

STEVE BARLOW ⇒ STEVE SKIDMORE
SANTY GUTIÉRREZ

Big baddie Mr Butt Hedd is in hot pursuit of the space cadets and has tracked them down for Lord Evil. But can Jet, Tip and Boo Hoo find a way to escape in a cunning disguise?

978 1 4451 5988 1

SPACE PIRATES

STEVE BARLOW ⇒ STEVE SKIDMORE
SANTY GUTIÉRREZ

Jet and Tip get a new command from Master Control to intercept some precious cargo. It's time to become space pirates!

978 1 4451 5979 9

WEB WORLD

STEVE BARLOW ⇒ STEVE SKIDMORE
SANTY GUTIÉRREZ

The goodies intercept a distress signal and race to the rescue. Then some 8-legged fiends appear ... Tip and Jet realise it's a trap!